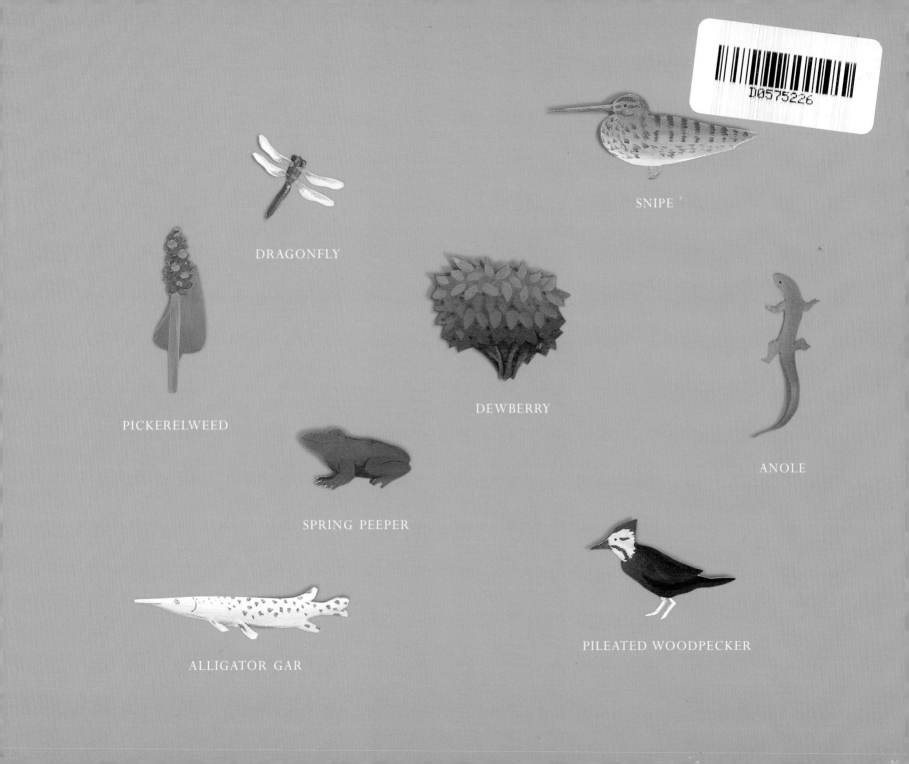

SNIPE

DRAGONFLY

PICKERELWEED

DEWBERRY

ANOLE

SPRING PEEPER

ALLIGATOR GAR

PILEATED WOODPECKER

To Judy and Bruno—such a sweet granmere,

such a fine granpere!—K.A.

For Shari. She's quite a special friend.—M.H.

Special thanks to C. C. Lockwood for his helpful advice

concerning the illustrations in this book.

For information on how you can help the Louisiana black bear, contact the Black Bear Conservation Committee, P.O. Box 83881, Baton Rouge, LA 70884, telephone (225) 763-5425, fax (225) 765-2607. Their website is www.BBCC.org • Where, Where Is Swamp Bear? • Text copyright © 2002 by Kathi Appelt • Illustrations copyright © 2002 by Megan Halsey • Printed in Hong Kong. All rights reserved. • www.harperchildrens.com • Library of Congress Cataloging-in-Publication Data • Appelt, Kathi, date. • Where, where is Swamp Bear? / by Kathi Appelt ; pictures by Megan Halsey. • p. cm. • Summary: While fishing with his grandfather in the swamp, a young boy asks all kinds of questions about a very special bear. • ISBN 0-688-17102-8 —— ISBN 0-688-17103-6 (lib. bdg.) • [1. Bears—Fiction. 2. Swamps—Fiction. 3. Grandfathers—Fiction.] I. Halsey, Megan, ill. II. Title. • PZ7.A6455 Wh 2002 00-033582 • [E]—dc21 CIP • AC • Typography by Stephanie Bart-Horvath • 1 2 3 4 5 6 7 8 9 10 • ❖ • First Edition

Where, Where Is Swamp Bear?

by KATHI APPELT
pictures by MEGAN HALSEY

HarperCollins*Publishers*

PIERRE: Granpere?

GRANPERE: Pierre?

PIERRE: Is this the place where Swamp Bear lives?

GRANPERE: It is.

PIERRE: But where? Where is Swamp Bear?

GRANPERE: Wherever her tracks fill up with water, as if she were never there.

PIERRE: Mine fill up, too! Look! My steps are full. Has Swamp Bear come this way?

GRANPERE: It's hard to say. Perhaps. I've heard she likes it, too, where the sun leaks through the treetops. That's where the berries like to grow.

PIERRE: Does she know they turn her tongue from pink to blue? What else does she do?

GRANPERE: She robs the bees.

PIERRE: She does?

GRANPERE: You see the ancient cypress stump? That's where the bees keep all their gold.

PIERRE: And do they swarm around her nose and buzz around her ears?

GRANPERE: So I'm told.

PIERRE: Granpere! Such a bear!

GRANPERE: Mmm. . . .

PIERRE: But where, where is Swamp Bear?

GRANPERE: Wherever there's a pine tree to use as a scratching post.

PIERRE: Not a sweet gum or a tupelo?

GRANPERE: I've heard she likes the pine trees most.

PIERRE: Granpere?

GRANPERE: Mon cher?

PIERRE: The water here is black as ink.

GRANPERE: The tannin from the leaves, I think. They fall into the slimy stew and then, like tea, they steep and brew. And when the water's dark as night, the mink can slink clean out of sight.

PIERRE: But . . . the swamp is just a little scary. . . .

GRANPERE: It's good to be a little wary.

PIERRE: Granpere, this bear, does she ever take a swim?

GRANPERE: She dives right in! And later, by the water's side, she watches for a perch to glide past her waiting paws.

PIERRE: Is she very, very quiet?

GRANPERE: I think so. Let's try it.

PIERRE: Granpere?

GRANPERE: Pierre?

PIERRE: The swamp is getting dark and deep. . . .

GRANPERE: A good spot for a bear to keep. Whisper now . . . not a peep. . . .

PIERRE: All those sounds, all those noises . . .

GRANPERE: The swamp has many, many voices. Now look up in that hickory tree and tell me—what else do you see?

PIERRE: A pair of owls! A green anole!

GRANPERE: The swamp is not so very lonely.

PIERRE: But it's so full of secret spaces, hidden nests, hiding places. Do you think Swamp Bear knows them all?

GRANPERE: I wouldn't be surprised a'tall.

PIERRE: Granpere?

GRANPERE: Pierre?

PIERRE: What else does Swamp Bear like to do?

GRANPERE: I've heard she likes to take a snooze way up in the arms of trees.

PIERRE: Way up there? Swamp Bear? But Granpere!

GRANPERE: Mon cher!

PIERRE: Do you think Swamp Bear knows we've come?

GRANPERE: She's quite a special bear, that one.

PIERRE: But where? Where has she been this whole long day?

GRANPERE: I can't say, but I have a feeling . . . she . . . isn't . . . far . . . away.

The bear that Pierre and Granpere are looking for is really a Louisiana black bear. She's a smaller subspecies of the North American black bear. One hundred fifty years ago, Louisiana black bears could be found throughout the state as well as in most of east Texas and all of Mississippi. Nowadays, they are mostly found in two areas of Louisiana: the Tensas River Basin and the Atchafalaya River Basin.

The Louisiana black bear is very shy and secretive, so the two swampy river basins are perfect places for her to live. They're full of hardwood forests and thick underbrush, giving her plenty of spots in which to hide.

There is a legend surrounding the Louisiana black bear. When Theodore Roosevelt was president of the United States, he went on a bear hunt in Mississippi. After three days without seeing a single bear, the dogs finally tracked down a very old male. The guides tied him to a tree and called for the president, but when Mr. Roosevelt saw the poor bear, he couldn't bring himself to shoot it.

A political cartoonist named Clifford Berryman heard about the story and drew a famous cartoon of Mr. Roosevelt and the bear. After that Mr. Berryman used the bear in other cartoons about the president. It wasn't long before people began thinking about the bear as a mascot for Teddy Roosevelt. One day a shopkeeper, Morris Michtom, put two stuffed bears made by his wife in his shop window. When he did this, he came up with an idea. Mr. Michtom asked President Roosevelt if he could call these toy bears "Teddy's bears."

Today, there are lots of teddy bears, but not so many Louisiana black bears. Because of overhunting more than a hundred years ago as well as the loss of the thick, swampy forests that they need for protection, they are now on the official endangered species list.

Pierre's bear needs our help. We can respond by conserving our natural forests and wilderness lands and by reclaiming some of the wetlands that were drained for farming and other uses.

And if you do decide to track down a bear, take your binoculars and keep a safe distance!

WOOD DUCK

COTTON MOUSE

BARRED OWL

CARP

SNAPPING TURTLE

BALD EAGLE

OTTER